INVESTIGATIONS FOR SMART TEENS

ISBN: 979-8385624799
First edition - March 2022

2023 © La Bibli des Ados - All rights reserved

«Any representation or reproduction in whole or in part without the consent of the author or his successors or assigns is unlawful. The same applies to translation, adaptation or transformation, arrangement or reproduction by any art or process whatsoever.»

Hello to you :)

Thank you for choosing « La Bibli des Ados » to get your brain working while playing detective!

"Investigations for Smart Teens" is a collection of 8 exciting detective stories where YOU are in the shoes of a real secret service investigator...

Do you have the skills required to catch the culprits who are still on the loose? You'll soon find out...

Have fun.

Who are we?

"La Bibli des Ados" is a collection of funny, original and sometimes offbeat books, strictly made for teenagers only!

If you like this kind of books, you will love all the others already released and those to come ;)

You can access our store by scanning the QR code directly with your smartphone's camera:

How to play?

Not so fast inspector! Don't you listen to the instructions? I know you're eager to show us the extent of your talents, but still... Let us explain how it all works.

The principle is quite simple: for each investigation, the plot will be told to you through an interrogation between you and the alleged culprits. Then, you will have access to some elements such as conversation extracts, administrative documents, newspaper articles, etc... which will allow you to confirm or not your initial intuition.

You will then find the solution to each story to verify that you were not mistaken.

Above all, take your time to analyze everything carefully! And if you need to, you have a page at the end of each investigation where you can take some notes, like real detectives do!

Go ahead, we won't keep you waiting any longer... it's up to you now!

OVERVIEW

Investigation 1: ADELE

P.5 - 14

Investigation 2: ARNAUD

P.15 - 24

Investigation 3: OPHELIA

P.25 - 34

Investigation 4: JEREMY

P.35 - 44

Investigation 5: JOCELYN

P.45 - 54

Investigation 6: LEONARD

P.55 - 64

Investigation 7: RODOLPHE

P.65 - 74

Investigation 8: CHLOE

P. 75 - 84

Give us your opinion!

P.85

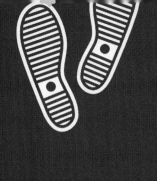

ADELE

INVESTIGATION 1: ADELE — Getting started

The military discipline that marked the boarding schools of the Theodore de Banville High School in Moulins has certainly become more flexible since the end of the nineteenth century, but it remains the SAS-norm (Sports Arts Studies) sections. Stamina, competition, and going beyond one's limits are the litany with which the boarders fall asleep at night and wake up in the morning. Except when the management authorizes the SPE, the spring break evenings, where music and alcohol are allowed, and illicit substances, consumed in moderation, are tolerated.

Adele LANGLOIS, like all the students, enjoyed the evening of the day before, but she did not wake up. The make-up marks on her pillow prove that she was smothered in her sleep. Her roommates, Louise GODART, Aïcha MANTOU and Joséphine FLAMONCOURT did not react when they saw the pillow on their friend's face, because this is how they always found her in the morning, because of the snoring of one of them. It was when they came back from breakfast that they realized that Adele had left school for good.

ME: How was last night?

LOUISE G. (in tears): Good! It was great! Adele was laughing and dancing. She was happy, like all of us. It was a very hard year. She worked like crazy. The exams were over, finally! She was my best friend since the sixth grade. We never left each other. (She bursts into tears)

ME: Ladies, can you confirm this?

JOSÉPHINE F. (frowning): Yes, I can confirm that! Adele, she was wild! That's what it's like when you're not used to drinking alcohol. She was so drunk that while dancing, she threw her glass in my face, this dumbass.

LOUISE G. (screaming): She didn't do it on purpose! And you know it!

JOSÉPHINE F.: I don't care! If you can't handle alcohol, you don't drink!

AÏCHA M. (tired): Oh shut up, Jo! Stop yelling like that!

You yourself were not fresh last night either.

JOSÉPHINE F.: Did anyone ask you for your opinion?

ME: Yes. I did. So Miss Jo wasn't fresh. What did you have?

JOSÉPHINE F.: Nothing special. Vodka, gin, tequila shots and beers. The usual.

ME: Did you all follow the same diet?

AÏCHA G.: In smaller amounts, for sure, but yes, we were all... very tired. In fact, on the way home, Louise took Adele's meds from her night table, in anticipation of this morning's headaches.

I take a look at the night table, whose drawer is still open. Indeed, they must have been very, very tired.

ME: Did you all come home at the same time?

LOUISE G. (aggressive): No! Only Adele, Aisha and me! When did you get home, Jo? We didn't hear you!

JOSÉPHINE F.: Hey girl! You are going to keep your voice down, you crybaby! Are you accusing me of something or am I dreaming?

AÏCHA M.: You did threaten Adele with a drink after she openly hit on your boyfriend in front of everyone.

LOUISE G.: Kevin was hitting on her! Not the other way around! It wasn't like Adele to do that!

ME: What time did you get home, Miss FLAMINCOURT?

JOSÉPHINE F.: Around 4 o'clock. I was with Kevin until then. I made it clear to him that I was much better than someone who's a virgin, like Adele. Do I have to draw you a picture as well?

LOUISE G.: You are disgusting Jo! Adele is dead and you have no respect for her.

JOSÉPHINE F.: Oh give me a break, Louise!

ME: Didn't you notice anything when you came into the room?

INVESTIGATION 1: ADELE — Getting started

JOSÉPHINE F.: *The only thing I saw was my bed. The rest didn't matter.*

ME: *Aside from the delightful and so altruistic Miss FLAMINCOURT here, did Adele have any enemies within the school.*

LOUISE G.: *Not at all. Adele was kindness personified. She got along with everyone. She was sweet and always willing to help. And if she had, she would have told me. She told me everything. We didn't hide anything from each other. She was sincerely appreciated, I can assure you that.*

JOSÉPHINE F.: *It's all relative, isn't it, Aïcha? Since she had grown up, you were no longer the school's VIP, not only with the students, but also with the teachers.*

AÏCHA G.: *Are you serious, Jo? You think I'd kill a rival just to be in first place?*

JOSÉPHINE F.: *Without a doubt. And I think that Solene GUIRAUD, to whom you poured a powerful laxative in her orange juice before the swimming exams, would agree with me. She still ended up in the emergency room.*

AÏCHA G.: *That was never proven!*

JOSÉPHINE F.: *No, but everyone knows it.*

ME: *Did Adele have a boyfriend?*

AÏCHA M. (mean): *Besides Kevin, you mean?*

JOSÉPHINE F. (ready to pounce): *I'm going to make choke on your medals!*

Louise then leaps to her feet and screams into the room.

LOUISE G.: *Stop it, both of you! I hate you! You're hysterical harpies, that's what you are! Three years that we've been sharing a room with you two. In a few weeks, Adele and I would have graduated and left that crazy school together. We were going to go to New York for our studies and we would have had our own apartment, both of us, in peace. She's dead and all you think about is yelling at each other for bullshit!*

ADELE

Aïcha and Joséphine fall silent, almost sheepish, and Louise returns to sit on her bed. She stares at Adele's bed, which is now empty, and calms down a little.

To answer your question, no, Adele did not have a boyfriend. It was just the two of us and our dreams. **She cries.**

I ask the girls to come out and let me inspect the room a bit. Something I have not been able to do until now. As soon as Adele's body was evacuated, her friends came into the room. Each bed has a small desk and a shelf next to it. Aïcha's bed is filled with cups and medals. Competitions won, whether in sports or beauty contests. The wall above Josephine's bed is filled with pictures of shirtless bikers with prominent abs. On Louise's desk, there is a photo frame where she and Adele are holding each other by the shoulders and making the victory sign with their fingers, a big smile on their lips. Adele's corner is dedicated to posters of Broadway shows. I'm rummaging through her bedside table. I find her diary and all sorts of generic, homeopathic and other medicines. A medical kit for all eventualities.

INVESTIGATION 1: ADELE — Brainstorming

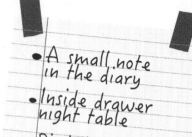

- A small note in the diary
- Inside drawer night table
- Disciplinary Board
- School results

THEODORE DE BANVILLE HIGH SCHOOL

12 avenue des éoliennes
03000 MOULINS
lyceebanville@banville.org
09 98 56 41 72

DISCIPLINARY COUNCIL REPORT
September 19, 2022

Persons present :
Joël DUBOUSIER, Director of the school
Armelle SANTONIN, Principal Education Advisor
Lénaïg GODEL, Head teacher
Rodrigue TURPIN, Class representative
Student concerned: Joséphine FLAMINCOURT

CHARGED FACTS:
Verbal and physical violence against a fellow student.
Damage to school equipment to the value of 4500,00 €
Insults towards his History Geography teacher
Consumption of alcohol outside the regulated periods

PENALTIES
Temporary exclusion of 8 days.
Reimbursement of school material within two weeks.
Upon return, the student will do 80 hours of general work in the school and meet with the psychologist twice a week until the end of the year.

Joël DUBOUSIER
Director

BFF
BEST FRIENDS FOREVER

"I love you"

MY SOULMATE
 A
 D
 E
 L
 E
MY LIFE

YOUR LOVE

THEODORE DE BANVILLE HIGH SCHOOL

Class of 2019 Ranking
First Quarters

STUDENTS	THEATER	DANCE	SWIMMING	CHEERLEADING
YEAR 2021 -2022				
Adele LANGLOIS	18/20	19/20	19/20	
Aïcha MANTOU	17/20	17/20	18/20	CAPTAIN
Solène GUIRAUD	15/20	16/20	16/20	Line 1
Anaïs DEBREY	15/20	16/20	16/20	Line 1
Stella ROCHEMONT	15/20	15/20	15/20	Line 2
Loïc TURSAN	14/20	14/20	14/20	Line 2
Rachel POIVRE	15/20	14/20	17/20	
Carla INDOUBET	14/20	14/20	15/20	Line 2
Dylan COURBET	14/20	14/20	14/20	Line 3
Coline JITOIN	13/20	13/20	13/20	Line 3
YEAR 2020-2021				
Aïcha MANTOU	17/20	17/20	18/20	CAPTAIN
Solène GUIRAUD	17/20	16/20	16/20	Line 1
Loïc TURSAN	17/20	17/20	16/20	
Adele LANGLOIS	16/20	15/20	17/20	
Carla INDOUBET	16/20	16/20	16/20	Line 2
Dylan COURBET	15/20	15/20	16/20	Line 2
Anaïs DEBREY	15/20	15/20	16/20	
Rachel POIVRE	15/20	14/20	15/20	Line 2
Coline JITOIN	14/20	14/20	14/20	Line 3
			13/20	Line 3
YEAR 2019-2020				
Aïcha MANTOU	17/20	17/20	17/20	CAPTAIN
Anaïs DEBREY	16/20	17/20	16/20	Line 1
Solène GUIRAUD	17/20	16/20	16/20	Line 1
Carla INDOUBET	16/20	16/20	15/20	Line 2
Loïc TURSAN	15/20	15/20	15/20	
Rachel POIVRE	15/20	15/20	15/20	
Dylan COURBET	15/20	15/20	15/20	Line 2
Adele LANGLOIS	14/20	15/20	15/20	
Coline JITOIN	13/20	13/20	13/20	Line 3
				Line 3

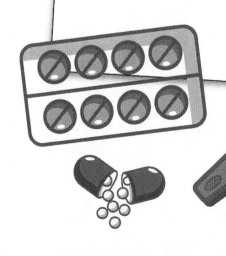

INVESTIGATION 1: ADELE   Case solved

The Director of the school allows me to use his office to see the girls again. Aïcha MANTON and Joséphine FLAMINCOURT seem to have finally understood the seriousness of the events. They are very calm and their reddened eyes wander around the room, as if they were looking for answers.

JOSÉPHINE F.: Louise...Forgive me for what I said earlier. Even though Adele wasn't my friend, I shouldn't have spoken like that...like it was just behind her back. I'm sorry for her death; I really am.

AÏCHA M.: Me too, forgive me Louise. I should never have insinuated anything between Kevin and Adele. I know she was only thinking about her studies, and especially her career on Broadway. It was childish and inappropriate. I can't believe she's gone.

LOUISE G.: ...No, she's not here anymore.

ME: So what happened last night that one of you decided to take the life of this young girl with a future?

AÏCHA M.: What? You think it was one of us?

JOSÉPHINE F.: You're crazy! It was a guy who did this! Holding a pillow over a face to smother a person takes a lot of strength! I saw this on a show. A guy came in while we were sleeping and killed Adele.

AÏCHA M.: But of course! That's the only way it could be! There have already been assaults in the rooms, several years ago.

JOSÉPHINE F.: Yes, it's true! I've heard about it. Adele was very pretty. Maybe she ignored a guy and he didn't like it!

AÏCHA G.: Exactly! He was so upset, and he killed her! There are crazy people everywhere, you know!

ME: So you think she was killed out of love?

JOSÉPHINE F.: Out of love, maybe not so much. But it doesn't take much to make you go crazy. And I'm in a good position to tell you this.

ADELE

ME: I was asking Louise. Louise? Was Adele killed for love? Or out of jealousy?

LOUISE G: I don't know...

ME: Was it the discovery of the pregnancy test in her drawer that disturbed you?

JOSÉPHINE F.: What?

LOUISE G.: We had decided to go to school in New York since the third grade. She dreamed of Broadway. She knew all the musicals. Outside of high school, she took singing lessons. She was good at it. At first, she was just a friend. My friend. We stuck together against the jerks. We studied together for classes. We liked the same movies, the same books. We were inseparable. Our feelings evolved. Mine, more than hers. She was afraid to admit to herself that she could love a girl. She had doubts. And then last year, she changed physically. She became even more beautiful. Her looks, her shape, her confidence evolved. Boys started to look at her and she liked it. She let herself be hit on; she enjoyed it. She felt that it was hurting me, so she reassured me that she had made her choice. She liked me, and it was just in good fun with the boys. But there were rumors about her being lighthearted. She didn't care at all. Last night she was glowing, and more than one guy approached her. We could barely go ten minutes without her being approached. But she didn't mind. I was sad and upset when we got home. She slumped on her bed and asked me to give her a pain reliever. And to Aïcha too. And then I saw the pregnancy test. Then I realized that the rumors were true. We went to bed. I tossed and turned in my bed. I couldn't fall asleep. I heard Jo come in. She started snoring immediately. I got up. I watched Adele sleep. As usual she had her pillow over her face. So I squeezed it. She was so drunk that she didn't struggle for long. She left me.

JOSÉPHINE F.: But Louise! It wasn't her pregnancy test, it was mine."

INVESTIGATION 1 : ADELE   Note-taking

ARNAUD

INVESTIGATION 2: ARNAUD — Getting started

Monday September 05, 2022

Seeing these people in white suits and their transparent helmets covering their faces, I almost feel like Neil Armstrong ready to climb into his rocket. However, I am not at the International Space Station, but in a research building in Bayonne. Jacques Goblin, Director of the institute, but above all, a friend, precedes me to a room closed by a huge metal door decorated with the yellow and black "radioactive" logo.

JACQUES G. (pale and agitated): We put the body here while we waited for you.

Through the small window, I can see a body covered with a sheet.

ME: What happened?

JACQUES G.: At 9:30 this morning, Professor Celine Besson triggered the security alarm. Through the intercom system she told us that her brother Arnaud had just died.

ME: Where is she now?

JACQUES G.: In an office upstairs, with the other two members of the team.

ME: Were these people also present at the time of the incident?

JACQUES G.: Yes indeed, professors Christine Pujol and Gaetan Lobart were there too. They underwent all the chemical tests. There is no sign of a virus.

ME: Why do you need my services?

JACQUES G.: Because the victim's blood tests show the presence of rat poison.

ME: Oh, that's too bad! The poor man must have suffered terribly.

ARNAUD

JACQUES G.: *He was an eminent professor, about to make a great discovery with his team. All 4 of them were ready to file a patent. The scientific world has been scrutinizing their work for years. Honestly, I don't imagine Arnaud Besson confusing powdered sugar with rat poison to drink his coffee. And I don't want the story to get out either, the press is on the lookout.*

ME: *I'll take care of it Jacques. You just relax.*

JACQUES G.: *Thank you.*

Jacques goes back to his office, a little relieved, while I enter the small room where Arnaud Besson lies. The photo on his badge shows a handsome man in his fifties, while his actual face is stained with vomit and blood. His eyes are wide open and I can give us a hint about the pain which overwhelmed him. Tears dried along his cheeks. Athletic, manicured, on the cusp of international fame, this man clearly doesn't fit into any of the boxes of the perfect suicide guide. Let's go interview his collaborators.

Standing in a corner of the office, leaning against the wall, a cup of water in her hand, I immediately recognize Celine Besson. She is the spitting image of her brother. Twins, no doubt.

CELINE B.: *Hello. Jacques told us about you. Why are we being held here? My brother just died and I'd like to...* **she bursts into tears.**

CHRISTINE P.: *Come and sit down Celine. Come with us.*

Gaetan Lobart pulls out a chair and the two of them sit down around Celine Besson. I observe them, one after the other. Christine and Celine's eyes are reddened by tears, Gaetan nervously runs his hand through his hair. They look at each other, sympathetic, embarrassed, anxious...

ME: *Well, I'll get straight to the point. Ms. Pujol? When did you leave Mr. Lobart for Mr. Besson?*

CHRISTINE P. (bewildered): *But...*

INVESTIGATION 2: ARNAUD — Getting started

ME: Your badge. It says Christine L. Pujol. From the way you look at Mr. Lobart, while twirling his wedding ring with his thumb, and the tan mark on the ring finger of your left hand, I imagine that your separation is recent. You cried as much as Mrs. Besson, if not more so...I conclude that you had a relationship with the victim.

GAETAN L (annoyed): We officially broke up last week. But I knew for months that she was cheating on me with Arnaud.

ME: And you put rat poison in her coffee this morning!

GAETAN L. (shocked): What nonsense! We've been working together for years and our research is almost finished. Even if he stole my wife, Arnaud was irreplaceable. We can't do anything without him.

ME: Okay. I found the victim's phone. Ms. Pujol, how did you react when Mr. Besson dumped you yesterday by text message?

CELINE B.: What?! He dumped you?! But why?

GAETAN L.: How? He broke up our marriage and then he dumped you? What a scumbag! ...Sorry, Celine.

CELINE B.: It's okay, Gaetan, I know how Arnaud could be sometimes...

CHRISTINE P.: I was very angry, as you can imagine. I tried to call him, but he never answered. I cried all night. This morning he totally ignored me. He started working as usual. As if we had always been just colleagues.

ME: And so you put rat poison in his coffee!

CHRISTINE P (annoyed): No, I didn't! And Arnaud didn't drink coffee! He was moody. We had already had arguments and break-ups, but it always worked out. Like every time, I hoped he would reconsider. I would never hurt him...I loved him too much.

There's a knock at the door. Jacques enters, embarrassed to disturb me during my interrogation, and slips a paper in my hands. He comes out immediately, just as embarrassed. I read it quickly.

ARNAUD

ME: Mr. Besson's autopsy revealed that his stomach contained aspirin.

GAETAN L.: Yes, it's true! He had a headache this morning. He went to get a pill from the lab's medicine cabinet.

ME: Did that happen often?

CELINE B.: No. But he went out last night...he must have been hitting the bottle.

ME: Were you with him?

CELINE B.: We live on the same floor.

ME: Have you two always done everything together?

CELINE B.: Yes... Identical twins. Same studies, same hobbies, same colleagues...We were inseparable.

ME: ...Additional tests were done on all your blood samples...and Mrs. Besson... I hate to tell you this, but, you too have rat poison in your body.

CELINE B. (panicked): What?!... But... but that's impossible! I can't feel anything! Am I going to die?!

INVESTIGATION 2: ARNAUD — Brainstorming

- Vet bill
- Indus Clean bill
- Newspaper article
- Patent

9th June 2022

HE ADMITS HAVING POISONED ABOUT FIFTY PETS

After a meticulous investigation by the police, the person responsible for the multiple rat poisonings of pets in the Kléber, Langevin and Spinoza neighborhoods, has finally been apprehended and incarcerated at the Bayonne penitentiary center. The reasons for his actions have not yet been given, but a psychiatric follow-up has been initiated.

FRENCH REPUBLIC

NISP
National Institute of Scientific Property

INVENTION PATENT IN THE RESEARCH FIELD

CERTIFICATE OF OWNERSHIP
Intellectual Property Code - Book IV

ISSUANCE DECISION

The Director General decides that the patent 96 07014 of the National Institute of Scientific Property, the forms of which are attached, is granted to ARNAUD BESSON.

The grant is effective for a period of twenty years from the date of filing of the application, i.e. June 15, 2022.

Mention of the grant will be made in the Official Bulletin of Scientific Property n° 98/33 of 22.06.2022. Its recognition has an international character.

Through this patent, Mr Arnaud Besson is the sole beneficiary of all future scientific benefits.

Made in Paris on 22.08.2022
EXECUTIVE DIRECTOR NISP

ARNAUD

Invoice 7584BAY

INDUS CLEAN
ZI Pallanquet–33000 BORDEAUX cedex2

Date
January 8, 2022

For
Research Institute
Quartier Duhalde
64100 BAYONNE

Recipient
Goblin Director

[Add additional instructions]

Quantity	Description	Unit price	Total
2	100 liter window cleaner canister	75,00	150,00
50	Dust bomb	25,00	1250,00
1	Industrial vacuum cleaner Roberto	450,00	450,00
4	GREENLOCK rat poison bag 20 kgs	43,00	172,00
25	Liquid black soap bottle 2 liters	29,00	725,00
100	Microfiber cloth 25x25 cm	12,50	
5	Cleaning team annual subscription		

LA FOUGÈRE Veterinary Clinic
8 Quartier des pins – 64100 BAYONNE
Phone 05 59 11 11 11 – contact@lafougere.bay

LA FOUGÈRE

29/04/2022

INVOICE 995874

BILLED TO
BESSON Arnaud
55 Avenue Foch
64100 BAYONNE

PATIENT
Buddy

ANIMAL
Cavalier King Charles dog

QUANTITY	DESCRIPTION	UNIT PRICE	TOTAL
1	Antidote injection for rat poison vitamin K1	75,00€	75,00€
3	Hospitalization under observation	110,00€	330,00€
1	Box of 10 Vit K1 vials	49,00€	49,00€

SUBTOTAL 454,00€

Thank you for your trust.

INVESTIGATION 2: ARNAUD — Case solved

It is now 5:00 pm. I asked Jacques to join us in the office with a security guard. The first one bites his nails, the second one blocks the door. The teachers are sitting across from me.

ME: Considering the possibility given to any citizen to consult the official scientific bulletins, I suppose that the three of you have seen that Mr. Besson has granted himself the glorious and economic benefits of your common research... This must have irritated you a bit, right?

GAETAN L. (furious): Yes, a lot! But we can't go back. Arnaud has locked everything up!

CHRISTINE P.: What he did is unforgivable...but that's the way he was.

CELINE B.: I took it as a betrayal...but as Christine says: "that's how he was".

ME: How is Buddy?

CELINE B. (surprised): Buddy? Fine, thank you. ...Oh my God Buddy! He'll be lost without Arnaud.

ME: This story of repeated poisoning in the city's neighborhoods is sordid. Good thing the culprit was arrested.

CHRISTINE P.: Yes, I remember when Arnaud had to rush Buddy to the vet. He was devastated.

GAETAN L.: We can know why we are talking about this stupid dog!

CHRISTINE P.: Gaetan! Please!

ME: Don't you like animals, Mr Lobart?

CELINE B (startled): Oh my God! Gaetan! ...you used that story to poison Buddy.

GAETAN L: What?!

CELINE B: Yes, you wanted to get back at Arnaud for Christine! You wanted to hurt him, I'm sure! And when you found out about the patent, it made you mad and you poisoned him this morning! And me too in the process, because you hate me!

GAETAN L.: But that's not right! You're completely crazy, my poor Celine! I would never do something like that! And I don't hate you!

ME: The rat poison found in Arnaud Besson's body was not only in his stomach, like the aspirin, but in every part of his body. Logic dictates that your brother had been ingesting a small but daily quantity of this poison for several months. His death could have taken place in several more weeks, but the aspirin intake caused a chemical shock that was fatal.

CELINE B. (to Christine and Gaetan): You saw Arnaud every day! You have premeditated his death, you monsters.

GAETAN L.: There you go again!

CHRISTINE P.: Because you're putting me in the mix now?

CELINE B.: Who else? Even I've been poisoned by you.

I applaud in the direction of Celine Besson.

ME: And the Oscar goes to Madame Besson! What an interpretation! Acting is the career you would have liked to follow if you hadn't been under the influence of your brother, isn't it? There is usually a dominant and a dominated one in identical twins. Worn out by Arnaud's personality for so many years, constantly in his shadow, the patent blow was the one too many. Thanks to the care you gave to Buddy during his hospitalization, you not only knew how to contain rat poison, vitamin K1, but you also had some in stock. So, day after day you administered the poison to your brother... once in his tea, once in his sandwich, once in a cupcake... Last night you knew he had been drinking and therefore would have a headache this morning. As a scientist, you were aware of the potential side effects of aspirin. So, this morning, you too ingested some rat poison, thus clearing yourself of suspicion, but you immediately reversed its effect by injecting yourself with a vitamin K1 vial, without anyone seeing. The police will certainly find a syringe in the container intended for this purpose. Do you have anything to add, Mrs. Besson?

CELINE B.: ...I should have been born first.

INVESTIGATION 2: ARNAUD

Note-taking

OPHELIA

INVESTIGATION 3: OPHELIA — Getting started

So many good memories at the Superior Law School Darrigrand in Ustarritz! The lecture halls, the student evenings, the exams, the love affairs... Famous names have passed through this establishment. Strong potentials are currently there. It is therefore with great surprise that Chantal Fournier, the Director, did not see one of the brilliant and promising students at this morning's Business Law exam... And for good reason, instead of working on her copy, Ophelia Gonnisset is lying on the floor of her room, her blond hair coagulated by blood. The liquid now cold, comes from a consequent wound at the back of the skull, apparently made with the corner of the laptop of the victim. This last one being put on the desk and Ophelia not being reputed to be contortionist, she obviously did not violently hit herself behind the head to give herself death, and then put back her working tool on the piece of furniture. She was helped to do so.

CHANTAL F: I thank you for your immediate availability. Since the construction of this school, you know that there has never been such incidents. I am devastated.

ME: Yes, I know the reputation of the school, and murder is not one of them.

CHANTAL F.: Can you help us? I want to keep the police out of this. At least until this is cleared up. Your discretion is legendary.

ME: I learned the value of it in this school, so I'll do my best. You told me that Ophelia has a study group this semester. Can you introduce me to it?

CHANTAL F: Yes, here they are.

Sitting at a table in the library, three students look in our direction, all the while tapping on their cell phones. Emotion is probably not what's choking them.

CHANTAL F: This is Samya Ottoman, Astrid Le Bihan and Estelle Marlaux. I'm going back to work. Call me on my mobile if you need anything. I give you the key to Ophelia's room. Please make sure you leave it locked. And thank you again for being here.

Chantal Fournier walks away while I sit down with the girls. At first glance, these three have nothing to do together; dress-code wise, I mean. Astrid shines brightly with her rhinestones, glittery nail polish and fake pastel pink Chanel suit, Samya hides under an oversized neon green hoodie, and Estelle's blue eyes are the only touch of color in her gothic outfit.

OPHELIA

ME: Hello ladies. How long has your study group been together?

SAMYA O: Since January.

ME: Were the four of you all hanging out before that?

ASTRID LB: Not at all. The draw brought us together. We have them every two months. It's to teach us how to work with all kinds of personalities.

ME: Yeah, I know. How do you three get along?

ESTELLE M: We each have our own personalities, but overall, yes, we get along well.

ME: And with Ophelia?

ESTELLE M: ...It was a little more complicated with Ophelia...She was a workaholic, and we're...cooler...

ASTRID LB: Yeah...we had some time to ourselves...we had some parties...

SAMYA O: Ophelia was all about her studies. She never went out. Sometimes she would have a drink, but never alcohol.

ESTELLE M (eyes to the sky): She was as straight as the law, all the time... "You shouldn't do this, you shouldn't do that"... a bit self-righteous around the edges

SAMYA O (adamant): Very psycho.

ASTRID LB: Ooooh yes!

ME: In short, it wasn't a great relationship!

ASTRID LB: That's right! But job-wise, she was very diligent and she was a great asset in that sense.

ME: When was the last time you saw her?

ASTRID LB: Last night. We were having drinks at the Campus Bar to relax before the midterm today.

ME: Did she say yes?

INVESTIGATION 3: OPHELIA — Getting started

ASTRID LB: That's right! But job-wise, she was very diligent and she was a great asset in that sense.

ME: When was the last time you saw her?

ASTRID LB: Last night. We were having drinks at the Campus Bar to relax before the midterm today.

ME: Did she say yes?

SAMYA O: We kind of obliged her, because it was the last time we worked together. The groups are being pulled out of the draw tomorrow.

ME: What time was that?

ESTELLE M: We met at 7 p.m.

ME: What was her state of mind?

SAMYA O.: Stressed, like everyone else before every midterm!

ESTELLE M.: Yes, but not only. She was also angry about the rumor.

ME: Which rumor?

ASTRID LB.: It seems that the exam subjects are sold on the sly a few days before. And as a result, some very mediocre students end up at the top of the list when the results come in. Ranking is very important here.

ESTELLE M: And Ophelia couldn't stand that. As we told you, she was a workaholic. She studied like crazy. Because she loved it, but also because she didn't want to lose her scholarship.

ME: Are you all on scholarship?

All three girls nod in agreement.

ME: Do you remember exactly what she said at the bar?

ASTRID LB.: She was pissed and swore that if she found out who was doing this school subject trafficking, she would report them. She couldn't stand the cheating, the ploy, the free rides. She had all the makings of a great lawyer.

OPHELIA

SAMYA O: Yes, it's true that she couldn't stand the injustice and couldn't imagine using illegal substances to cope.

ME: Is there a amphetamine traffic in the school?

ESTELLE M: She didn't have proof, but everyone knows. Isn't that right, Samya?

SAMYA O: Oh shut up Estelle! You know I stopped that! Thanks to Ophelia, by the way.

ME: What do you mean?

SAMYA: She yelled at me non-stop for thirty minutes. Even my own parents never lectured me like that. Rules were Ophelia's drugs.

ESTELLE M: I was also the victim of her ruthlessness when I had the misfortune to admit that I had managed to cheat on a sports grade in high school. I thought she was going to crucify me on the spot.

ME: What about you, Astrid? Did you manage to avoid God's judgment?

ASTRID LB: Uh...if you will...I had to be careful about who I dated, shall we say... Anyway, she was intangible.

ME: And not everyone must have liked it... How did the evening end?

SAMYA O: Quietly. 8:30 pm was the limit we gave ourselves to be in shape this morning. Astrid paid, it was her turn, and we went back to the dormitory.

ESTELLE M.: But on the way, we talked a little bit with some students that Ophelia suspected of cheating...

ASTRID LB: And even though she had finally calmed down at the bar, her thirst for justice took over.

SAMYA O: Yeah. She was just as mad as she was at the beginning of the night when we got back to the dorm.

INVESTIGATION 3: OPHELIA — Brainstorming

I have had to deal with witnesses who were shocked by a murder and who, to protect themselves, distanced themselves from the event. But here, these three young women answered my questions, as if nothing had happened. It's almost like I was bothering them in the course of their day. That's the kind of behaviour that seems strange to me. That's why...I'm still searching.

- Partial ranking December 2021
- Bar note
- Exam copy
- Office letter

Law firm
HEXOAK & MANEX
72 Avenue Robert Malraux
75015 PARIS

To Superior Law School DARRIGRAND
Damoiseau Park
64480 USTARRITZ

Paris, April 18, 2022.

Dear Fournier Director,

In view of the various resumes you have sent us, we have selected two candidates for the two-month internship, during the summer of 2022, in our premises. Namely, Mrs. Ophelia GONISSET and Estelle MARLAUX.

We are waiting for the results of the end of year exams, to make our final decision.

Sincerely yours.

F. HEXOAK

Law Office HEXOAK & MANEX – 72 Avenue Robert Malraux 75015 PARIS – Phone: 01 49 78 52 31 – cabhexman@free.fr

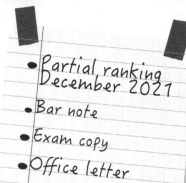

Astrid Le Bihan

ID: DROIT INTERNATIONAL

11/20

You can do much better than that, my little sweetie. Come by my apartment so I can give you private lessons again tonight at 8pm!

OPHELIA

CAMPUS BAR

05/05/2022

	Unit price	Total
2 Caipirinha	12,00€	24,00€
2 Piña colada	15,00€	30,00€
2 Mojitos	9,50€	19,00€
1 Sparkling water	6,00€	6,00€
1 Mint water	4,50€	4,50€

Total owed: 83,50€
Payment: In cash

Thank you for your visit!

INTERNATIONAL LAW TEST RESULTS
DECEMBER 2021

1	HUIRET	Céline
2	RACOUT	Christophe
3	OTTOMAN	Samya
4	DUPERT	Yvan
5	ETCHEGARAY	Txomin
6	PORIET	Erwan
7	GONISSET	Ophelia
8	LIMOTOU	Sophie
9	NALOTTE	Mathilde
10	FICART	Laurent
11	RIVIERE	Enzo
12	SEGUIN	Claire
13	URQUIA	Bixente
14	LAPARRA	Amaïa
15	DOMENGER	Eva
16	CODMARD	Joséphine
17	PICCOLLI	Clara
18	ZOUMIER	Julie
19	LEBIHAN	Astrid
20	SOUPIAN	Rodolphe
21	DELGONDO	Lubin
22	CROUZET	Pablo
23	MALRAUX	Estelle
24	CAMBON	Emma
25	GILLES	Yaël
26	DEMESTRES	Mahé
27	CHAPIROUX	Prune
28	PORTAL	Cyrielle
29	MONTAUD	Yoan
30	BURIL	Max
31	HALLAUX	Jade

INVESTIGATION 3: OPHELIA — Case solved

At the end of the day, I meet the girls and Director Fournier in the latter's office. This time, the students have the decency to leave their phones in their bags and pretend to listen to me carefully.

ME: In your foursome, I was able to discern the profile of each one. First of all, there is the Meritorious One, Samya, who, in view of her copy this morning, without chemical help, because I believe her completely when she says she has stopped everything, has known how to use her brain to the best advantage.

SAMYA O: Oh yeah, I quit! And I worked like crazy, with Ophelia's methods. *(looking at the Director)* Is it true, did I get a good grade?

CHANTAL F.: I'd say your grade is honorable... But we'll have to discuss the chemical aid together...

ME: Then there's Opportunist Astrid, who is in a relationship with a faculty member.

ASTRID LB: But I love Jean-Jacques!

ME: It's obvious...

CHANTAL F.: What?! Which Jean-Jacques? LEMONIER ? BELFORT ? XEBAST? But come on! You cannot sleep with your teacher!

ASTRID LB.: I'm of age and your rules are obsolete!

ME: Then there's the normal one, Estelle, in the sense that she works dutifully and, even if her December results are not the highest, her personality and her resume have won over the lawyers of a prestigious firm.

ESTELLE M.: Thank you, but I'll never know if they took me for myself or because my competitor died.

ME: And finally, there was The Smart one, Ophelia, who by her perspicacity, understood that to pay a bar bill of 83,50 €, in cash when you have a scholarship...it's suspicious! Isn't it Astrid? Trading exam subjects is quite lucrative it seems...

ASTRID LB.: It was an accident!

OPHELIA

ME: The computer fell on the back of Ophelia's head by itself?

ASTRID LB.: On the way home from the bar, when we met the students she suspected of cheating, she realized that I knew them, a little too well. I went to her room and we talked. She lectured me, again, and was determined to go to Madame Fournier. Things got heated and with the alcohol, I hit her with her computer. She fell down and I left.

ME: And this morning, as if nothing had happened, you took your exam, and as usual, you partially passed so as not to arouse suspicion.

ASTRID LB: Opportunistic AND smart!

INVESTIGATION 3 : OPHELIA — Note-taking

JEREMY

INVESTIGATION 4: JEREMY Getting started

I am at the bedside of Jeremy POULON, a divorce lawyer, in room 207 of the Lapeyronie hospital in Montpellier. This forty-eight year old man was found, by chance, by a walker in the Domaine de Grammont at the northern exit of the city, in the morning. Intrigued by the presence of a car in this secluded corner of the forest, Jean-Yves Broussard inspected the dilapidated hut that was next door. Inside, tied to a chair, blindfolded and with a paper bag over his head, Jeremy Poulon was dying. Since then, with his arms perfused, he has opened his eyes a few times, only to fall back into a deep sleep. I am waiting for his relatives to find out more. A knock at the door. The nurse precedes a woman in her forties with dark circles around her eyes, who shouts when she sees Jeremy.

ISABELLE T.: Oh my God!

NURSE: Don't worry, the bruises on his face are an allergic reaction to the paper on his head. It will gradually fade. His lungs were affected, but he will recover. He was lucky that this walker found him. A few more hours and he would have asphyxiated. On the other hand, he was beaten repeatedly. I'll leave you to it.

The nurse leaves, leaving the door open.

ME: Mrs. Poulon I presume?

ISABELLE T.: Ex Mrs. Poulon. Isabelle Taucat from now on, and this is our son Yoan.

A teenager of about fifteen enters then, his eyes red, but not only because of tears, considering the yellowish tips of his fingers. The last cigarette he smoked must not have been all tobacco.

YOAN P.: Oh damn, Dad!

And finally, a man also in his forties walks slowly through the door and looks relieved to see the patient.

OLIVIER C.: Jeremy!

JEREMY

OLIVIER C.: I am Olivier Circès, Jeremy's best friend and colleague. We've known each other since childhood. I'm also Yoan's godfather.

ME: Why didn't any of you report Mr. Poulon's disappearance?

ISABELLE T.: Because I didn't know he was missing. The police called me this morning to tell me he was in the hospital. Friday evening I left Yoan in the parking lot of the Fougerolles supermarket at 6:00 p.m. and went back to work. Jeremy had to pick him up as usual. It's the school vacations. He had custody of his son for a week. They were going to go to Ibiza together.

YOAN: That's what he told you, Mom. But for several months he had signed me up for a sailing course for this vacation. He had decided to go alone.

ISABELLE T.: What? But why didn't you tell me?

YOAN P.: Not to worry you.

ME: And to have a quiet week, without parents around.

YOAN P.: Also...

ISABELLE T.: Did you know about this, Olivier?

OLIVIER C.: No, I didn't! Jeremy had told me about Ibiza with Yoan, too.

ME: Your best friend is keeping secrets from you, it seems.

OLIVIER C.: I guess so.

ME: When was the last time you all saw him?

ISABELLE T.: It must be at least six months ago. Since the divorce, we've only exchanged short text messages.

ME: What about you Yoan? When was the last time you saw your father?

YOAN P.: Saturday afternoon. He dropped me off at the water sports center and left right away because his plane was at 3:20.

ME: Mr. Circès?

INVESTIGATION 4: JEREMY — Getting started

OLIVIER C.: *Friday night. We went to pick up Yoan with my car. We carpool, and this week I was the driver. We picked up Yoan and I dropped them off in front of their building before going back home. Right Yoyo?*

YOAN P: *Don't call me that! Yeah, we got home just in time for my show.*

ME: *Okay. So on Saturday afternoon, Mr. Poulon didn't get on his plane, but went to the Grammont forest with his car. Why did he do that? Good question! Given his current state, as soon as he gets there, he gets knocked out, judging by the bump on the back of his head, and is tied to a chair. It is Thursday. That makes four and a half days of sequestration. A few pieces of stale bread and a bowl of stagnant water on the floor of the cabin suggest that Jeremy's torturer wanted to give him a hard time.*

At that moment, the patient slowly opened his eyes and looked around. When he saw his loved ones, tears streamed down his cheeks. He tries to say something, but immediately falls back to sleep. Yoan is holding back tears too.

OLIVIER C.: *They had to fill him with painkillers.*

He comes towards Isabelle Taucat who starts to tremble. He takes her in his arms, while Yoan chews on the sleeves of his too-big-for-him sweater.

OLIVIER C.: *It's okay, it's okay, Isa.*

ME: *Have you two known each other for a long time?*

OLIVIER C.: *Yes, but not as long as with Jeremy. The three of us met in our senior year. We were both in love with Isa, but she chose Jeremy.*

ISABELLE T. (smiling gently): *It was difficult, you looked so much alike!*

Same look, same size, same craziness...But Jeremy had that little extra spark at the time that made me fall in love.

ME: *What were the reasons for your divorce?*

ISABELLE T.: *Over the years, Jeremy became bossy and moody. The birth of Yoan didn't help. He became jealous of his son and constantly put me down.*

JEREMY

We divorced a year ago. He doesn't accept it and makes my life hell.

ME: What do you mean?

ISABELLE T.: I have to work three jobs to take care of myself and my son. I hardly sleep, I see Yoan a few hours a week, but I'm always the person to contact in case of emergency!

ME: And you and Mr. Circès found each other?

OLIVIER C: Not in the way you might think. We're just friends. Really good old friends. And I don't understand why Jeremy treats Isa like that. It's unbearable!

ISABELLE T.: Forget it, Olivier. I know there's nothing you can do, and I don't want to get in the way of your friendship.

ME: Did you know of any enemies?

OLIVIER C.: Grumpy customers, you think?

ME: Why not...

OLIVIER C.: I can't think of any. I'm sorry. But I can ask around.

Jeremy moves his left hand. There is a shock in the room. Isabelle clings to Olivier even more and Yoan bites his nails furiously. The patient's hand slowly falls back on the sheets and the regular beeping of his heart activity invades the atmosphere again. The tension is palpable. A little too much, in fact.

At the end of the day, Jeremy Poulon finally wakes up. Visibly shocked, he is unable to say a word and all my questions remain unanswered. The night will serve as a cradle for my investigations and, I'll bet, will bring me the solution.

INVESTIGATION 4: JEREMY — Brainstorming

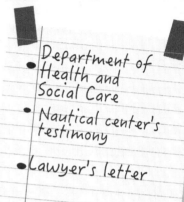

- Department of Health and Social Care
- Nautical center's testimony
- Lawyer's letter

00:51, 214.9KB

(TELEPHONE CONVERSATION)

NAUTICAL CENTER VALRAS BEACH: *Nautical Center of Valras, hello?*

ME: *Good morning, sir. In the framework of a judicial investigation, I would like to ask you some questions about Yoan Poulon.*

NCVB: *Yoyo? The little Poulon kid? What's wrong with him? Nothing serious I hope! He's a sweet kid. He wasn't here this morning.*

ME: *No, don't worry, he's fine. He's at his father's bedside in the hospital.*

NCVB: *Oh my! Jeremy?! What happened to him? An accident?*

ME: *Sort of. Did you see Monsieur Poulon early Saturday afternoon?*

NCVB: *Well, yes, he brought the kid in for the sailing course that was starting.*

ME: *Did you talk to him? Did he seem okay?*

NCVB: *No, I didn't talk to him. He was in the parking lot and I was in the office. We waved at each other. And yes, he looked good to me! Damn! Yoan told me he was going to Ibiza for a week. He already had the complete tourist's starter kit! The cap and the dark glasses! Even though it was very cloudy. What a show-off that guy was!*

ME: *Well, thank you.*

NCVB: *Say hi to him for me.*

JEREMY

LAW OFFICE BEAULIEU
Lawyer Laurine Beaulieu
12 Place de la Comédie
34000 MONTPELLIER

Montpellier,
March 12th 2022

TO VALMONT & ASSOCIATES OFFICE
Lawyer Robert Lemonier
8 Allée Corbusier
34820 TEYRAN

Case AK703B POULON/TAUCAT POULON

Dear colleague,

At the request of my client Isabelle TAUCAT, I come back to you, once again, to ask for the setting up of a mediation between the former POULON spouses. The financial situation of my client is very precarious, and her physical and mental health are suffering from it.

Thank you for reiterating this request to your client Mr. Jeremy POULON.

All my best regards, dear colleague.

Ms. Laurine Beaulieu
Lawyer

HERAULT'S DEPARTMENTAL COUNCIL
AND
HERAULT'S DEPARTMENTAL DIRECTION OF SANITARY AND SOCIAL SERVICES

Montpellier,
March 9, 1982

Following the signs of abuse inflicted by Mr. Jean-Claude ████ to his wards, his accreditation as a foster family has been withdrawn. He is currently being referred to the Public Prosecutor's Office for an aggravated case of violence against minors.

The children, Jeremy POULON and Olivier CIRCÈS, aged 9, have been temporarily placed in the "Marie Crissargues's Kids" institute, in Carnon.

Commission Director

DDSS 29 Bd Elysee Saisset 34000 MONTPELLIER. Phone: 51 53 47 12 Fax: 51 53 47 14

INVESTIGATION 4: JEREMY — Case solved

It is Friday. It is 2:00 pm. Mr. Poulon is wide awake; his bed is a little bit higher, but he still can't talk. His relatives enter the room. Moved, he starts to cry again. Everyone smiles at him and sits down wherever they can.

ME: This is a very unusual case, ladies and gentlemen. First of all, and this is not to my displeasure, because the victim is alive. Also, because there are several victims, in different degrees, as well as several culprits.

First of all, Mrs. Taucat, victim of her ex-husband, expert in divorce, who by the means of the law, which he knows on the end of the fingers, ties her hands so that she has to work to raise their son correctly. We can see a symbolic metaphor with the ties that held Mr. Poulon to his chair.

ISABELLE T.: What?! But you're delirious! I had nothing to do with it!

ME: Then there are two other victims. Two little 9 year old boys who for months suffered the abuse of a surrogate father, in foster care: Jeremy Poulon and Olivier Circès. This terrible period united you for life. Injustice destined you to study law. Mr. Circès specialized in social affairs.

OLIVIER C.: That's all set in the past.

ME: Not so much. Let me tell the story, and you can stop me if I'm wrong. Annoyed by Jeremy's attitude toward his ex-wife, and your former childhood sweetheart, you ask him to join you at the Grammont estate for some sort of problem. Like a good best friend, Jeremy rushes over to you. There you knock him out and tie him to that chair for several days. A little punishment between friends. Am I right?

OLIVIER C.: Yes, that's right!

ISABELLE T.: Olivier! No !

ME: Beep! The lady is right when she says "no", because it's not the real story... When did you understand Mr. Circès?

ISABELLE T.: Understood what? What are we talking about?

ME: Understood that Jeremy Poulon was beating his son, your godson...

ISABELLE T. (horrified): What?!!! What kind of story is that? Yoan, it's not true! Say something!

JEREMY

Yoan bows his head and turns back to the window without saying a word.

ISABELLE T.: *But that's impossible! I would have seen it!*

OLIVIER C.: *When, Isa? When would you have seen it? You spend all your time working. You come home very late, exhausted. Yoan is already asleep and you leave in the morning very early. You said it yourself, you see him a few hours during the week.*

ISABELLE T (in tears).: *But...*

YOAN P.: *It's not your fault, Mom.*

ME: *Go on, Mr. Circès.*

OLIVIER C.: *First I noticed that Yoan was smoking cannabis. His pupils were often dilated, and the smell too. I tried to talk to him about it, but he said it was just to be like the others. And then he started wearing very large sweatshirts, too large for him. That's how Jeremy and I used to hide our bruises when we were kids. I saw us again, tied to chairs with this man who beat us, supposedly to teach us how to live. So I decided to act. Effectively, brutally, to make Jeremy remember what he had been through and that he had to stop. And it happened just like you said.*

ME: *No, not quite. If it was just a buddy fight, you wouldn't have had to blindfold Mr. Poulon and put a paper bag over his head. He was not supposed to see or feel the person who came with you to visit him.*

And when Mr. Poulon finally decided to talk, he told us that his ordeal began on Friday evening. Because Saturday afternoon, it was not him who accompanied Yoan to the nautical center, but you, with his cap and his glasses. The illusion was perfect, you look so alike.

So as I was saying, there are several victims. All of you, and several culprits, all of you as well, because even if Mrs. Taucat did not participate in the sequestration of her ex-husband, the guilt already invades her for not having seen the distress of her son.

JEREMY P. (in tears): *...I am sorry...*

INVESTIGATION 4: JEREMY

Note-taking

JOCELYN

INVESTIGATION 5: JOCELYN — Getting started

Private gulf, swimming pool of almost Olympic dimensions, 450 square meter villa with 100 square meter carport. All BUGATTI, of course, because this luxurious haven belongs to the family of the famous manufacturer of the cars of the same name. Such an extraordinary environment necessarily implied an equally extraordinary death for one of the young heirs. Thus, at 10 o'clock this morning, the body of Jocelyn BUGATTI, 19 years old, lay on the patio, overlooking the Arcachon pond. The arrow planted in his heart killed him instantly.

In the gigantic adjacent living room, the victim's girlfriend Amanda STERNEUVE, his younger brother Wilfried BUGATTI and his friend and teammate in the French national archery team, Lucas PLESSIN, are waiting. Wilfried BUGATTI, who has just poured himself a glass of champagne, sits down comfortably in his club chair.

WILFRIED B.: So? Is he really dead or is he playing the big Act 2 scene?

ME: Your brother is indeed dead, Mr. BUGATTI. You don't seem to be moved by the situation.

WILFRIED B.: As they say, "The King is dead, long live the King"!

AMANDA S.: Will! You're overreacting! It's tragic what's happened. Especially since we're all suspects, since we all know how to use a bow. Is there any more champagne?

ME: You don't seem to be traumatized by the situation either.

AMANDA S.: Oh me, you know, death has become a friend. My parents died in a car accident when I was eight. My aunt who took me in died of cancer last year and my grandfather is terminally ill. Not to mention the number of friends who have died from drug overdoses... Sometimes I wonder if I'm not cursed. (she laughs). One death more or less, as long as there's money in my accounts, I'm fine.

ME: You're not saying anything, Mr. PLESSIN.

LUCAS P. (pale): Why are you here? We have to call the police! Someone killed Jocelyn. Why don't you call the police?

ME: Consider me as such. Jocelyn and Wilfried's father requested my

presence as soon as he was informed of the drama by the housekeeper. I know how to be discreet, so I'm conducting this investigation until he arrives.

WILFRIED B.: Oh wonderful! Dad is cutting short his stay in London, because his darling son has died. I wonder if he would have done the same for me.

AMANDA S.: Will, honey, you already know the answer.

WILFRIED B (laughing): No, of course, he wouldn't.

LUCAS P.: For God's sake, Will, stop making it all about you! Joce is fucking dead!

AMANDA S.: Hey, calm down Lucas! Everyone reacts as they can. And maybe now Will will finally get his father's attention.

WILFRIED B.: Yeah, man, let me deal with my grief in my own way. Just because you get along with your sister like a rock, doesn't mean it's the same in every family.

LUCAS P.: Leave my sister out of this, will you?!

AMANDA S.: Oh no Will, you hit the nail on the head. Little Lucas is worried about his poor little sister in a coma...how sad. Plus this night was supposed to cheer you up, right? Tighten one more cup for me Will, please.

LUCAS P.: You fucking...

ME: Hop hop hop, let's all calm down here! Miss STERNEUVE, I don't know if this cynical and hateful attitude is fake or natural, but in any case, I would ask you to show a little more civility in the given context.

Mr. PLESSIN, why is your sister in a coma, if you don't mind me asking?

LUCAS P.: She has had a heart condition since birth. She had a few warnings in the last years, small attacks, but nothing too serious. But last month, after her swim practice, she had a bigger one and was put in an induced coma...

INVESTIGATION 5: JOCELYN — Getting started

WILFRIED B.: This is the first night Lucas has spent with us since. Joce came up with the idea for this little moment between the 4 of us, to take his mind off it. Sorry buddy, I didn't mean to remind you of this.

AMANDA S.: No hard feelings Lulu. You know I can be a real bitch sometimes. Cheers.

ME: Are the parties here usually more ... impressive?

WILFRIED B.: Oh yeah! It's at least a hundred guests with a DJ and bouncers at the gates of the property.

AMANDA S.: Last night, Joce wanted more simplicity, more intimacy, for her faithful friend Lucas. That's so sweet.

LUCAS P.: Seriously, what's your problem, Amanda? You couldn't stand that I was his best friend? That I got to know him before you started dating him? That he had someone in his life other than you to rely on? In that case, maybe I should have been the one to get shot!

ME: Let's not go astray, young people. So it was in your honor that Mr. BUGATTI had organized this little meeting?

LUCAS P.: Yes, that was it. It was really nice, this little party between us. It did me good. I can't believe he's dead. What the hell happened last night?

ME: Can you explain to me how the evening went, please?

WILFRIED B.: Nothing unusual. Lucas and Amanda came in around 8:00. We had a drink and then we all went to practice on the shooting range behind the pool.

AMANDA S.: Jocelyn was in great shape. He almost beat me. But as usual, I won the most points.

ME: Did you sense his concern?

LUCAS P.: Not at all! He was looking forward to the next national competition. He was very confident in our team.

JOCELYN

WILFRIED B.: Then we went home. The servants served dinner and went home.

LUCAS P: The four of us watched a movie.

AMANDA S: And then Joce went to get some champagne and his own personal booster.

ME: What's this personal booster?

WILFRIED B: Space cakes.

ME: Really?

LUCAS P.: Yes. Every time we win, we have a party and Joce makes space cakes to celebrate. And like I said, he was very confident about the next competition.

AMANDA S.: So confident that we got his last recipe, as well as his last win.

ME: What do you mean?

WILFRIED B.: He added a little oxycodone to the flour.

LUCAS P.: Oh, we got high!

AMANDA S: And then we went to bed. And we found him on the patio when we got up.

This disillusioned golden youth who fueled by champagne as breakfast is frankly confusing. Not to mention the space cake stuffed with opioids to celebrate a sports victory. Has the drug/alcohol combo awakened a criminal instinct in these clueless youngsters of high society?

INVESTIGATION 5: JOCELYN — Brainstorming

- Interview with Réginald Bugatti
- Newspaper article Amanda
- Guest list

(INTERVIEW IN THE PROGRAM "THE SMALL POND")

Live from Nice. It is with a big smile that Reginald BUGATTI was holding the gold cup of the individual archery competition, won by his eldest son Jocelyn, at the exit of the locker rooms. He gave us a short interview:

RB: "My son Jocelyn is my greatest pride! He excels in everything! He has gold in his hands, and his mind is platinum! My worthy successor, no doubt about it."

LPB: "Your youngest son Wilfried also made his mark in fencing. He won the bronze medal."

RB: "Fencing is a sport for rednecks."

LPB: "Are you going to celebrate these victories with your family?"

RB: "I'm taking Jocelyn to the Ritz tonight. My jet is waiting for both of us."

It seems that Mr. BUGATTI's personal plane is a two-seater.

JOCELYN

VICTORY PARTY LA ROCHELLE GUESTS

NAME		NAME		NAME	
ABOU	V	GUSINI	T	VANGUE	M
ABRION	G	HERAUD	R	VENEL	N
ACCETTI	N	HIRIART	M	VERNEUIL	V
ACHOIT	H	HUBERT	M	VILLIERE	C
ARCHAMBON	T	HISTRAC	F	VOULUIR	A
ARTICOU	R	JAVA	B	YGINSKY	R
ASTIER	S	JAVERT	J	ZORIA	T
BALIVON	R	JINOIN	K	ZUGASTI	O
BARDOS	T	JOULES	L		
BENET	O	JUTALO	L		
BIOLET	P	KARKI	O		
BONIFACE	L	KERENSAC	P		
BONNEFONT	L	KLEBER	A		
BOSPHORE	J	LAPARRA	D		
BURGAT	D	LARTIGUES	E		
CAZUERTA	A	LENOIR	T		
CEROLA	X	LEVEQUE	S		
CIHALE	C	LOPEZ	C		
COJARE	C	MABRE	C		
CUFFIN	D	MANUTO	H		
DARANTXA	S	MERIAC	J		
DARRIERE	R	MUDIN	M		
DERFOUR	K	OLIVARO	G		
DIFFENTHAL	M	PALESO	A		
DOMINGUEZ	C	PATUREL	S		
DONGUE	L	PEDESTRIA	F		
EBAN	F	PIRLOT	T		
EDIMBURG	H	PLESSIN	L		
EDIVER	A	PLESSIN	K		
EGOLUE	S	POTIN	R		
ENFANT	F	PRATT	E		
FABERGE	M	QUERTUDEZ	D		
FAURE	M	RAMENEZ	G		
FETUCCI	R	RIVIERE	U		
FICHE	V	ROLAND	O		
FOULET	S	RUFFINEL	L		
FROUART	G	SAINT-JEAN	H		
GADILAC	J	SAUVAIRE	F		
GARRIGRAND	V	SIKAVIK	C		
GIRARD	B	SITRUS	S		
GLAIN	N	STERNEUVE	A		
GNAFOT	X	STRENEL	R		
OERTY	A	TARIN	A		
ONZALEZ	E	TERTRE			
JERIN	J	TO...			

People
THE MOST GLAMOROUS JET SET COUPLE IS STILL ON EVERYONE'S LIPS!

On 3 October, Jocelyn BUGATTI literally devoured the mouth of fashionable model Lorenza Cruzot in front of the fashion week cameras. Amanda STERNEUVE, his girlfriend, was quick to react by rolling a tank over her ex-partner's car.

The latter, amazed by the panache of this revenge, showed up at Amanda's home with red roses imported from Italy to make up for it.

The couple are now on a Caribbean cruise for a fortnight.

There have been countless break-ups between these two! For now, they are together and happy. Let's hope that the saying "Love stories always end badly" does not apply to them.

INVESTIGATION 5 : JOCELYN   Case solved

After showers that must have used up half the Indian Ocean, the three clichés of the wealthy bourgeoisie join me in the living room. The servants have cleared away the remnants of the previous evening's party, replacing them with a brunch worthy of the White House.

ME: A fratricide, that would look good in the press, wouldn't it? What do you think Mr. BUGATTI?

WILFRIED B.: I think it would be stupid! Because I will go to prison with an even greater hatred of my dear father towards me. I won't be able to enjoy my new status as an only son on whom his affection would finally be poured. And finally, the inheritance would pass me by! Any other relevant questions?

ME: No. Your logic, devoid of all feelings, is unstoppable, I agree. Mr. PLESSIN, on the other hand...

AMANDA S.: Lucas? The guy that wouldn't kill a fly? You're joking! Apart from crying at his sister's bedside, he can barely watch Bambi without shedding a tear, so to commit a murder...

ME: You're definitely an idiot, Miss STERNEUVE, at any time of the day. Mr. PLESSIN, would you please explain your gesture.

LUCAS P.: Kiera...

AMANDA S.: Again with your sister...

ME: Shut your big mouth, Amanda, it'll be a vacation!

LUCAS P.: Kiera was there at the last party. Like all of them, and...

AMANDA S.: What? She was in love with Jocelyn, right? And then?

ME: How about a big slap across your painted-on bitch face? With or without momentum? I'll give you a choice!

WILFRIED B.: Shut up Amanda! Go ahead Lucas, we're listening.

JOCELYN

LUCAS P.: Yesterday, when Jocelyn said that he had put oxycodone in his space cake, and especially that he had tested this recipe since the last night of the victory against La Rochelle, without telling anyone, I made the connection. I didn't have any that night, I didn't want to. Neither did Kiera, but she had brought some in her bag. The next day, after her swimming training, she took a space cake as a snack and apparently, the oxycodone was fatal to her. This opioid is not compatible with her heart condition. Cannabis may have medical benefits, but not oxycodone. Jocelyn should have warned us. He was my best friend, but because of him, my little sister might die. So, certainly boosted by his magic cakes, I took my bow and offered him a little night training. He liked the idea and followed me. And I shot an arrow in his heart.

INVESTIGATION 5 : JOCELYN

Note-taking

LEONARD

INVESTIGATION 6: LEONARD

Getting started

With the relentless use of his screwdriver, Emile, the concierge of the Grand Hotel of Bordeaux, finally managed to open the bathroom door of the largest suite.

The splendid 105 m² room was rented by the famous novelist Leonard HERMIONE. This young author, with his admirable writing, undoubtedly deserves the Pulitzer Award with his latest work "Just once", which has sold millions of copies. However, given the writer's inert body, eyes wide open, in the gigantic octagonal bathtub, the award will be given posthumously.

Everything leads us to believe that Mr. HERMIONE drowned. Yes, drowned in barely thirty centimeters of water, perfumed with island vanilla scent. In a room that he had taken time to close, that said, from the inside, with three people in the next door's living room. Cécile PELONGE, his partner; Eric BORNE, a journalist and Steve DELORME, the victim's assistant.

ME: And you didn't hear anything?

CÉCILE P. (in tears): Absolutely nothing! I didn't even know anything was going on!

ME: Was it usual for Mr. HERMIONE to take a bath while other people were waiting in the next room?

STEVE D.: It was a long day at the book signing. Leo wanted to relax a bit before giving an interview to Mr. BORNE.

Eric BORNE (panicked): This is terrible! Leo, dead! It can't be true! *(to Cecile Pelonge and Steve Delorme)* It's a set-up, right? It's just a set-up to unravel the next novel! Say it! Say it, damn it!

Eyes bulging, breathless, the journalist is on the verge of a panic attack. Against all expectations, logic would have wanted Mr. DELORME to bring him a glass of water or possibly alcohol, to put him back on his feet; but instead, the latter suddenly shouts "LERVAC" and jumps on the scribbler, as if possessed by the devil. He falls on the ground and almost hits his head on the coffee table. Cecile Pelonge, hysterical, takes a magazine and starts to hit Eric Borne, as if he was the biggest mouse she had ever seen.

LEONARD

Then Emile, the janitor, intervenes, and using him body as a shield, prevents any further attack on the journalist.

STEVE D.: Lervac! You bastard! You've no right to be here, you crazy bastard! Cécile! Call the police!

ME: Easy, peasy! The police is here.

CÉCILE P: You didn't move!

ME: Please forgive my surprise, but I wasn't expecting this little fight. And Emile handled it very well.

EMILY: Just like in the good old days, Chief!

ME: Thank you, my friend! Now, can you explain this emotional outburst to me?

STEVE D: This guy is not a journalist. He's a fan of Leo. A guy who's totally unhinged and has been stalking him for years. Who has sent him hundreds of letters. First adoration, then death threats.

CÉCILE P: He followed us several times while we were walking, in his car. He kept watch at the foot of our building for days and nights on end. He is no longer allowed to approach us. The judge ordered a restraining order against him after he held Leo for over an hour in a restaurant bathroom last year.

Eric BORNE LERVAC then stands up. The curly black wig, now askew, reveals smooth blond hair. Once the hairpiece is removed, it is a greasy catogan that adorns the head of the fanatic. He then takes off his little black goatee, also fake, and removes his blue contact lenses, which reveals two little black eyes full of madness. I'll have to ask him where he gets his makeup, because these items are bluffing of natural. I admire the makeup artist.

ERIC B. (repeating several times): Well, it's a staged scene! He's not dead! He's not dead!

ME: Now shut up, Two-Face! Emile, please go and have a look in the bathroom, and check the garbage can.

EMILE: Right away!

INVESTIGATION 6: LEONARD — Getting started

STEVE D.: *This guy needs to be locked up, I'm telling you! He was harassing Leo! He even threatened me because I was his assistant and he wanted to take my place.*

ERIC B.: *Of course! You're a notorious incompetent! A leech who uses Leo to promote himself and asks him to correct his bland scripts.*

STEVE D.: *You asshole!*

ME: *STOOOP! Stop or I'll knock and I'll make sure you don't get up, either one of you.*

CÉCILE P.: *Steve? You know Leo and I were wondering if that guy caused your accident last year?*

ME: *Dear little lady, I don't think that's the impression to give right now, considering the state of Mr. DELORME's nerves…But, that being said, one, I reiterate my warning as to the violence of which I am capable of, and two, Mr. DELORME, which accident is "Ms. Adding-Fuel-on-the-Fire" over here talking about?*

STEVE D: *Eleven months ago, a car hit me while I was crossing at a crosswalk. The driver got away and I was in a coma for a little over nine months.*

ERIC B: *I had nothing to do with that! The police questioned me. I was in Orleans that day and witnesses confirmed it.*

CÉCILE P: *You could have paid someone to do it, you degenerate!*

ME: *That's enough, Mrs Pelonge! You're sharpening people's minds a bit too much with your interventions!*

ERIC B: *Degenerate, me? Who was on the front page of all the newspapers because she attacked Leo with a knife? Was it me?*

CÉCILE P.: *(hysterically) It was an accident! Just an argument that went wrong!*

ERIC B: *Yes, that's right, everyone is arguing with a knife at hand.*

LEONARD

Just then, Emile returns with a napkin in his hand.

EMILY: Look what I found, Chief.

He opens the towel and shows us an insulin syringe and a small bottle. I take the latter and sniff it after opening it.

ME: Which of you knew that Mr. HERMIONE was diabetic?

CÉCILE P: Everyone knew. Leo said it in an interview several years ago.

ME: Who went into the bathroom before Mr. HERMIONE went to take his bath?

STEVE D: I went in there when we were coming up from the book signing.

CÉCILE P: I went upstairs an hour before to take a shower. And the other nutcase took pictures of the whole room, including the bathroom, for his so-called story.

ERIC B. : Do you know what the Nutcase is going to tell you.

I won't go on about the Nutcase's left middle finger movement towards the Lady...

ME: Emile? Is this the only bottle of insulin you could find?

EMILY: Yes, Boss!

ME: Now I understand why Mr. HERMIONE didn't make a sound when he died.

STEVE D.: Why?

ME: Because it wasn't insulin he injected to himself, but curare. A dreaded poison that paralyzes muscles. Used in small doses as an anaesthetic, it must be coupled with respiratory assistance to avoid any movement during a surgical operation. There, in this bottle labeled "insulin", it's actually pure curare, which he put in his veins. Totally paralyzed, he didn't move, couldn't call for anyone, choked and died in total silence.

INVESTIGATION 6 : LEONARD — Brainstorming

- Mail from Steve to Leonard
- Newspaper article
- Restraining order

THE KNIVES ARE OUT — People

The most glamorous couple in the literary world is in the news again this week. Indeed, Cécile Pelonge was taken into custody for having attacked Leonard Hermione, her partner of eight years, with a knife. The latter, taken to the emergency room, was left with a six centimetre gash in his left arm. However, he refuses to file a complaint against his beloved, whose moods he knows. It is however the second time that this kind of incident happens within the couple. In her defence, Cécile Pelonge quoted "He said he wanted to leave me. We've been together for eight years! I have put up with everything! The lean years, with his unsuccessful books, his depression. And now that he's hit the big time with his latest book, he wants to dump me? That's crazy!"

It was under the influence of alcohol mixed with drugs that Cécile Pelonge said all this. Her lawyer, used to his client's addictive outbursts, tells us not to give importance to her allegations. Nevertheless, one could wonder if the saying "love stories always end badly" can be applied to this sulfurous relationship.

Nathel.B

Thanks for your corrections   16/07/2021 22:47

Steve Delorme (steved@gmail.com) Add contact

To Leonard HERMIONE

📄 *Primeure.pdf*

Hi Leo,

This is my latest draft, after the corrections you advised me to make.

I hope to be as successful as you.

See you tomorrow at the office.

Good night.

Steve

LEONARD

We are here to help you N° 15458*05

FRENCH REPUBLIC
MINISTRY OF JUSTICE

cerfa

Application to the family court judge for the issuance of a protection order

(Article 515-9 and following of the Civil Code, Articles 1136-3 and following of the Code of Civil Procedure)

Your identity:

Your last name: HERMIONE
Your usual name (e.g. husband's / wife's name):
Your first name(s): LÉONARD
Your date of birth: |1 |4|1 |1|1|1 |9|9|1|5
Your place of birth: LIMOGES
Your nationality: FRENCH
Votre occupation: WRITER
Your e-mail address: leonardhermione@free.fr
Your phone number: 07 25 88 74 69

Defendant's identity:

His/her last name: LERVAC
His/her first name(s): NOËL
His/her date of birth: |2 |7|1 |2|1 |1|9 |9|1|4|
His/her place of birth: ORLÉANS
His/her phone number: |0 |7 |3 |9 |2 |0 |5 |4 |1 |6 |1
His/her address: 8 RUE FORT DE LA BROUSSE 75015 PARIS

■ The indefinite prohibition in time, for the defendant to get closer to you unless from a 500 meters distance.

SWORN STATEMENT

I, the undersigned (first name and last name): HERMIONE LÉONARD
hereby certify that the information provided on this form is correct.

On 04 :04 :2021

Done in: PARIS

Signature

61

INVESTIGATION 6 : LEONARD   Case solved

After the funeral home has evacuated the body of Leonard HERMIONE, in the greatest discretion, I go down with the three suspects in the lobby of the hotel. The rococo style of the bar seems to me to be a good place to confound the murderer of the successful author. Each of them is sitting in a comfortable chair and is waiting for me to speak up.

ME: In a homicide, the victim's spouse always get looked at first. Please don't get carried away, Ms. Pelonge. Even if you have a particularly sulfurous personality, you are more the type to act on a whim, and moreover, with a knife. To each his method.

Mr. BORNE, alias Noël LERVAC is more into provocation than action. The use of hairpieces shows his taste for staging. He would never have attempted to kill the one who inspired him and whom he admired. That leaves you, Mr. DELORME. We are listening to you.

STEVE D.: I lost nine months of my life because of this accident. Nine months! When I finally woke up, I was completely alone. The nurses told me that a few friends came to see me, at first...but after a while, they lost hope and mostly had other things to do. Even Leo stopped coming to see me. My mentor, my friend with whom I had worked for over five years. I learned to walk again with long rehabilitation sessions. Still alone. Yet Leo knew I was out of the coma. I called him, but he never came. The conversation barely lasted ten seconds. Then one day, the nurse who was taking care of me brought me his book "Just Once" because she knew that Leo was my friend. From the first lines, I knew. I understood why Leo had cut me out of his life. It was my script that he edited, and he signed it with his own name. That fame should have been mine. I got out of the hospital and went to see him. We got to talking.

STEVE D.: Hey Leo, how are you?

LEONARD H.: You're the one to ask, big guy. I missed you so much!

STEVE D.: But you haven't come to see me since I called you when I came out of my coma.

LEONARD H.: I'm sorry, but you know how it is...

STEVE D.: No, I don't know. Explain it to me.

LEONARD

LEONARD H.: Look, I understand that you could be mad at me, but I had your script edited for you, because it was great. It needed to see the light of day.

STEVE D.: So if it was for me, why is it your name on it?

LEONARD H.: Well, so it would sell even better. This way, I could pay for your hospital bills indefinitely.

STEVE D.: Forgive me for waking up from my coma too soon then.

LEONARD H.: Don't be silly, Steve. I was very shocked by what happened to you. I lost my inspiration for weeks. That damn blank page syndrome! But now you're here, and it's wonderful!

STEVE D.: But how are you going to set the record straight now?

LEONARD H.: Steve...you know I can't. I can't say now that you're the real author of "Just Once". It's too late. Especially since I have a shot at the Pulitzer.

STEVE D.: You have a chance for the Pulitzer?

Leonard H.: You know what I mean, my man. And it's better this way, Steve. You're still psychologically fragile. Such notoriety, all at once, would have been too much for you. You'll write another masterpiece, I'm sure.

STEVE D.: After this discussion I felt even more alone. I went back to my assistant job, but I had lost all faith in Leo, in life in general. I thought about getting rid of myself. So I asked around and curare seemed to be a good solution. Paralyzing, a bit like it was during my coma, but conscious. I bought a bottle of pure curare on the Darkweb. I always had it with me and I also knew I could use one of Leonard's syringes. That signing day in Bordeaux was the one too many. All those fans I had to take a picture with Leo for the novel I had written. When I went to the bathroom to wash my hands, I had decided to get it over with. Then I thought about what Leo had said to me: "You'll write another masterpiece, I'm sure". So I decided to listen to him, and I will write it in prison. It will sell even better that way.

INVESTIGATION 6 : LEONARD

Note-taking

RODOLPHE

INVESTIGATION 7: RODOLPHE — Getting started

It is all excited that Charles POIS, old friend of my parents, welcomes me at the doors of his retirement home "The blue hummingbirds", a few kilometers from Gueret. It is with great pleasure that I visit him, especially since today, Joris, his grandson, is doing a theater performance with his company, in the facility. The common room has been arranged so that the two hundred or so residents and half of the staff can attend the show. I was given a reserved seat in the front row. The play, written by Tristan CHAPUIS, also director, is a drama tinged with black humor, which puts forward two male roles, Joris POIS and Rodolphe LEROY. The actors are screaming with truth in this victim / narcissistic pervert exchange, and the consequences of such a relationship. After an hour and forty-five minutes of scathing dialogue, the victim, played by Joris, finally finds the solution to his ordeal by stabbing his psychological torturer. It is a thunder of applause which invades then the retirement home, followed after a few moments by the shrill cry of Fanny DELGADO, the make-up artist and costume designer. Rodolphe LEROY is still on the floor, a pool of blood spreading under his belly. He just played his last performance.

JORIS P. (bewildered): What's going on? Why isn't Rodolphe getting up? And why did you add a bag of fake blood, Fanny? We said last time that it didn't add anything to the play. Rodolphe! Rodolphe! Get up, for god's sake! Stop acting like an idiot!

With the greatest calm, the nurses lead the residents back to their apartments. Only Joris POIS, Charles, who wants to support his grandson, Tristan CHAPUIS and Fanny DELGADO remain in the room.

ME: Who is in charge of the props in your theater company?

TRISTAN C.: It's Fanny. But there are only 4 of us, well 3 now, and each one of us does a little bit of everything.

ME: Ms. DELGADO, did you work on the props today, especially the murder weapon?

FANNY D. (shocked): ...

ME: Mrs. DELGADO? You are in shock. A nurse will bring you a glass of water, and maybe a sedative. But in the meantime, can you please

RODOLPHE

answer my question?

FANNY D: Yes... Yes, I've put all the props in their place, as usual. But, it's the wrong knife. The one in the room is a dummy, with a retractable blade. I don't know how that knife got there, I swear!

ME: Joris? You probably don't remember me because you were very young, but I know your grandfather well.

JORIS P. (leaning against Charles): Yes, I know who you are.

ME: This isn't the first time you've done this play. Didn't you realize the knife was different?

JORIS P: No. We have to have four or five different knives in total, just to make sure we don't run out, in case we misplace one. And honestly, I just pick it up mechanically, without thinking, and especially always in my role.

TRISTAN C.: The role of Joris is very heavy and emotional. He can't afford to let go of his character for a second. He takes the prepared prop and then that's it.

ME: Did other people have access to the backstage before the performance?

FANNY D.: They had a little lounge that was available to us as a dressing room. Anybody could go backstage.

TRISTAN C.: As usual, anyone who wanted to talk to us before the show started was welcome. We talked to several residents. In particular, Mr. POIS.

CHARLES P. (sad): Yes. I wanted to see Joris to give him a hug and wish him luck, and also to introduce him to my new girlfriend Doris.

JORIS P.: Doris will remember our first meeting just like I do, Grandpa.

ME: What was your relationship with Mr. LEROY?

INVESTIGATION 7: RODOLPHE — Getting started

TRISTAN C: More than just a good comedian whom I often called upon, Rodolphe was a long-time friend. He was my son's godfather and we saw each other regularly outside the theater. It's going to be a shock for my family and the theater family too.

FANNY D.: I haven't been a member of the company for very long. I met Rodolphe when the rehearsals started, about a year ago. I'm more in the administrative part, so I didn't see him much. Except for makeup and props.

ME: And how was he?

FANNY D.: A perfectionist.

ME: In what way?

FANNY D.: Every accessory in its place, makeup not too much, not too little; he could make me do it over and over again. He also liked to know that everything was in order in the paperwork.

TRISTAN C.: Yes, it's true that he could have that little "plus plus" side. But that's what made him so talented. Even with you Joris, he was uncompromising.

JORIS P.: Yes, that's true. He took his role very much to heart and could behave like his character, to get the best interpretation from me.

ME: You mean off stage he would belittle you and call you names like in the play?

JORIS P.: That was his way of working. You had to be in character 24 hours a day to be at your best.

ME: And you put up with that?

JORIS P.: He made me progress. My game is better. Tristan, you agree, right?

TRISTAN C.: Yes, it's undeniable, your character has taken on another dimension. But you were already very talented since the beginning, Joris. Be sure of that.

INVESTIGATION 7: RODOLPHE — Brainstorming

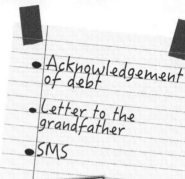

- Acknowledgement of debt
- Letter to the grandfather
- SMS

Paris,
01.09.22.

Hi Grandpa,

I am so happy to come play in your retirement home in a month. I'm really looking forward to meeting your Doris, which you've talked so much about.

I took your advice and went back to my psychiatrist. He increased my amount of anxiolytics and antidepressants. He is afraid that I might get another psychotic episode from all the pressure Rodolphe is putting on me. I don't want to go back to a psychiatric hospital. Never again!

So I hang on Grandpa!

Anyway, I know it's for my own good that Rodolphe is so hard with me. Tristan doesn't say anything, which means he's ok with it. But he hasn't been saying much for a while. It's as if it was Rodolphe running the gang.

Even Fanny is strange. It's like she's afraid of him.

But I'm hanging on Grandpa!

I'm giving you a big kiss.
See you soon.

Joris!

RODOLPHE

> So, my little slut? Have you thought about my proposal? Either you're very nice to me, or you lose your job.

> You know how it works in the business my little Fanny... give and take.

> What if you put make-up all over your body, my little Fanny?

> Did my kiss take you by surprise? Admit that you were waiting for it...

DEBT RECOGNITION

I, the undersigned Tristan CHAPUIS, born on 24/03/1977 in Paris and residing at 18 rue Louise, 75015 Paris, hereby acknowledge that I owe Rodolphe LEROY, born on 18/04/75 in Paris and residing at 55 rue de Vaugirard, the sum of fifty-five thousand euros (55,000 euros).

I undertake to fully reimburse this debt in one or more payments no later than 01/10/2022.

Made in Paris, on 01/10/2021.

Two copies available.

Creditor's signature

Debtor's signature

INVESTIGATION 7: RODOLPHE — Case solved

After inspecting the actors' dressing rooms and in particular the prop trunk, where several dummy knives are indeed stored, I ask the members of the troupe, as well as Charles, still supporting his grandson, to join me.

ME: Ms. DELGADO, when did the sexual harassment of Mr. LEROY begin?

JORIS P.: What? Rodolphe was harassing you, Fanny?

FANNY D. (embarrassed): Only a month after we started rehearsals. At first, it was a bit of heavy flirting, but then he started to flood me with text messages to get me to go out with him. The messages turned into sexting, and several times he cornered me in places in the theater. Each time I managed to get out of the way, but he became threatening, especially about my job.

JORIS P.: But why didn't you tell Tristan about it? He would have put him in his place!

ME: Nothing is less sure. Isn't that right, Mr. CHAPUIS? You knew very well how Rodolphe LEROY was treating Mrs. DELGADO. But you didn't say anything, as for the way he directed Joris, so that he played his character according to his personal vision of the play.

FANNY D.: Did you know, Tristan? Did you know? But why didn't you intervene, either for me or for Joris?

ME: Because he owed Mr. Leroy money. Fifty-five thousand euros to be exact. And I suppose that today, the final deadline for your acknowledgement of debt, you were still unable to pay him back?

TRISTAN C.: No, indeed, I couldn't pay him back and he knew it. Rodolphe was out of control. He had me, and he took advantage of that to do whatever he wanted with the troupe. He went after Fanny and Joris. But I couldn't say anything. I'm sorry. But I didn't kill him! I swear to you!

ME: You all had motive and opportunity to steal that knife and make Joris kill Mr. LEROY in front of more than 250 spectators. And by the way, very nice staging! Who would believe that an assassin would be stupid enough to commit a murder in front of so many witnesses?

RODOLPHE

JORIS P.: You're crazy! Rodolphe was an asshole, yes, he was! But not to the point of killing him! I've already been in a psychiatric hospital for violent acts, but on myself, and I wouldn't go back to those gnarly places for anything in the world!

FANNY D.: I didn't do anything either! I was determined to go to the police and file a complaint against Rodolphe!

ME: Please calm down, ladies and gentlemen. I said you all had a motive and an opportunity to replace that knife. You're not the only ones in this room as far as I know. Isn't it, Charles?

CHARLES P.: Wow, your parents did tell me you were incredible.

JORIS P.: Grandpa? What are you talking about?

CHARLES P.: I had to do something about it, son. Rodolphe was slowly destroying you; he was pushing you to your limits. He was abusing your sensibilities in the name of some kind of fair play that was on the edge of sadism. He was a bad guy, and there was no way he was going to make you suffer, like you suffered a few years ago.

Forgive me big guy, and please take care of my Doris.

INVESTIGATION 7 : RODOLPHE

Note-taking

CHLOE

INVESTIGATION 8: CHLOE

Getting started

Either Jeanine PICHARD, the little seventy-five year old lady in front of me, is in a state of shock, or she doesn't have light on all the floors. Or she is a sociopathic manic-depressive who has just slit her neighbour's throat. Or all three. In fact, she has been explaining to me for ten minutes now how to get a bloodstain out of carpet. But as things stand, it's not a stain, but a pool of blood that's spreading under the body of Chloe MARCHIN, a young twenty-year-old bride, in her garden-level flat in the suburbs of Lille. Hélène LEMERLE, the victim's home English teacher, livid, sitting on a chair in the dining room, is also starting to get tired with those cleaning lessons. As for Quentin GARTOIS, the victim's ex, he has been vomiting for the past ten minutes in the bathroom next door.

ME: Stooop! Mrs PICHARD please, stop!

JEANINE P.: I'm saying all this for the next tenants. Because I can imagine that Mr MARCHIN is going to move out after such a drama. And at the same time, the real estate agency certainly has an outstanding cleaning team to deal with this kind of situation. But...

ME: That's not the most important thing right now, you know. What were you doing in the victim's flat?

JEANINE P.: I was bringing the girl a product to improve the soil in her garden. I had already told her how to do it, but she wasn't listening! Youth! Nothing in the brain! Don't take care of your rosebushes properly, and you'll be invaded by fleas, you know. So...

ME: Stooooop! How did you get in? The door to the flat is locked.

JEANINE P.: Through the garden, of course. The building is built in such a way that it's easier to get in from the outside. All the ground floors in the residence do that. And I found the little one like that.

ME: You've never seen anyone go through their garden before?

JEANINE P.: No! I have my morning routine. I get up, have breakfast, clean up, wash up and then I open my shutter at 8.30am sharp. It's like that every day.

ME: Okay. Ms. LEMERLE, at what time did you arrive?

CHLOE

HÉLÈNE L.: At 10:00. The class was at 10:00 this morning.

ME: How long have you been teaching English to Chloe MARCHIN?

HÉLÈNE L.: It's been two months now, three times a week. She and her husband had to move to Australia for his work, and Chloe had very little command of the English language. But by the way, does Mr. MARCHIN know about what happened to his wife?

ME: Yes. I talked to him on the phone. He's on the first plane out of Sydney later today.

Hélène L.: Poor guy! He must be devastated. They had just gotten married, Chloe told me. What a tragedy!

ME: Did you know Mr. MARCHIN?

HÉLÈNE P.: No, I've never seen him. He left for Australia just before my classes started with his wife.

At that moment, white as a sheet and with exaggerated eyes, Mr. GARTOIS comes out from the bathroom.

ME: You should sit down, young man.

He sits down.

QUENTIN G.: Where is Chloe?

ME: Her body has been evacuated to the Forensic Institute. What are you doing at your ex-girlfriend's house, Mr. Gartois?

QUENTIN G.: To tell her that she was doing something stupid!

ME: Like what?

QUENTIN G.: Going to Australia.

ME: How is that stupid? She was simply following her husband.

QUENTIN G.: That was a mistake too! She should never have married that moron! She'd only known him for six months!

INVESTIGATION 8: CHLOE — Getting started

JEANINE P.: *It's called love at first sight, you young runt!*

QUENTIN P.: *I didn't ask for your opinion!*

JEANINE P.: *And rude too! Every time you came by, Chloe was in tears! You were hurting her, you idiot! And apparently, the beating you received from Mr MARCHIN didn't calm you down in your stupidity! Oh no! Since Kevin left, this little lout has been harassing Chloe almost every day! And then she came to my house to whine! How many times did she stop me from watching my TV series! Damn, it made me so angry! The best thing would be if the flat wasn't rented again. Then I'd finally have some peace and quiet. By the way, if you could make it short, it's almost time for my cooking show.*

QUENTIN P.: *Is she ever going to shut up!*

ME: *Calm down! You were trying to get Chloe back, weren't you?*

QUENTIN G.: *We were made for each other! We were together for three years! We met in high school. And then one day, she dumped me, out of the blue, for this guy!*

HÉLÈNE L.: *Allow me to intervene, but Chloe confided in me and the relationship with this young man was very tumultuous. He hit her several times and when I came to my class a fortnight ago, I could see that Chloe was terrified. I was the one who had to get him out.*

QUENTIN G.: *I didn't do anything to her! I didn't kill her! I loved her!*

CHLOE

INVESTIGATION 8: CHLOE

Brainstorming

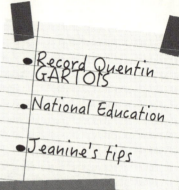

- Record Quentin GARTOIS
- National Education
- Jeanine's tips

TIPS FOR A BEAUTIFUL GARDEN!

1. Prune **REGULARLY** with pruning shears! No kitchen shears!

2. Mow your lawn **REGULARLY** with a mechanical mower. It's quiet and environmentally friendly!

3. Take care of the soil **REGULARLY**

4. Grow herbs! It will save you the trouble of buying them!

5. Install a mini pond! It's good for the birds!

6. Take care of the rose bushes I gave you!

7. I hate lavender, so use lemon to repel ants!

If needed, I'm next door, starting from 08:30!

Jeanine

CHLOE

FRENCH REPUBLIC
MINISTRY OF JUSTICE AND LIBERTIES
Directorate of Criminal Affairs and Pardons
National Criminal Record
123 rue Nationale 59034 LILLE CEDEX

NAME: GARTOIS
FIRST NAME: Quentin Lionel
SON/DAUGHTER OF: GARTOIS Christophe
AND GARTOIS Karine
IN Lille
BORN ON: 27/12/2002
LAST KNOWN ADDRESS: 27 rue La Bohème. Residency Clairefontaine 59000 LILLE
CIVIL STATUS: Single
OCCUPATION: Unemployed
NATIONALITY: French

Dates of convictions	COURTS or tribunals	TYPE of crimes or offences	SPECIFIC DATES of the crimes or offences	TYPE and length of penalties	COMMENTS
2018	Correctional Court	Violence against minors	12/12/2018	2 months of community service	Follow-up in a juvenile center
2019	Correctional Court	Pickpocketing	14/03/2019	Reminder of the law	One month detention in a juvenile center
2019	Correctional Court	Organized gang brawl	24/04/2019	Penal composition	Six months detention in juvenile center
2020	Criminal Court	Burglary	25/06/2020	2 months of conditional sentence	
2021	Criminal Court	Suspected of trafficking drug	21/10/2021	Reminder of the law	Testimony of this girlfriend in his favor

The Magistrate in charge of the National Criminal Record

ADMINISTRATIVE COURT OF LILLE

N° 1002060, 1003755

Mrs. HOTÉGUY Marie-Hélène / Nation...

Mr. Chamborette
Court reporter

Mr. De Pourcel
Public Court Reporter

Hearing of May 29, 2015

In view of the petition registered on April 30, 2015 under number 10002060, submitted by ...ycée Champollion de Lille, the removal from the National Education system of Ms. Marie-...élène HOTÉGUY, French and Modern Language teacher, on the grounds of inappropriate ...havior toward a student, is hereby confirmed.

INVESTIGATION 8 : CHLOE — Case solved

It is in the kitchen, far from the bloodstain which has become an obsession for Jeanine PICHARD, that I'm gathering the protagonists of this crime scene. Jeanine, always the shameless one, has poured herself a coffee and sits down on one of the bar stools.

JEANINE P.: Don't just stand there. Take a seat! The girl's not going to tell you anything now that she's dead.

ME: You were playing the authoritarian grandmother with Mrs MARCHIN, weren't you?

JEANINE P.: Well...they were a cute little couple. I didn't mind giving them a little advice.

ME: Advice like the ones for the garden? That sounds more like a military list.

JEANINE P.: I had to, otherwise she wouldn't understand, this little girl. She wasn't the sharpest tool in the shed.

QUENTIN G.: Don't you dare badmouth Chloe, you old hag!

ME: Mrs Lemerle, what did you think of Chloe?

HÉLÈNE L.: She was a nice girl. Indeed, perhaps not the most resourceful, but she put a lot of goodwill into my classes. She wanted to be at the top for Australia and for Kevin.

ME: Kevin?

HÉLÈNE L (confused)..: Yes Kevin... Mr MARCHIN... Her husband.

ME: And if not, when exactly did you want to kill her, tell me?

HÉLÈNE L. (defensively): I beg your pardon?

ME: Oh, come on! Jeanine is going to miss her show. Let's wrap this up! Your real name is Marie-Hélène and your former married name is HOTÉGUY. You were disbarred from the National Education system seven years ago, for, and I quote, "inappropriate behaviour towards a pupil. That pupil was Kévin MARCHIN, isn't it?

CHLOE

HÉLÈNE L.: Kévin turned 18 in his final year of high school. He was of age when our relationship started.

ME: That's what you told your superiors, but there's no evidence that it didn't start before. How long did your relationship last?

HÉLÈNE L.: Seven years! Seven beautiful years of happiness, until he met that little brainless idiot!

ME: The famous seven-year mark! The naïve girl has taken the place of the mature woman in Kevin's heart...

HÉLÈNE L.: Chloe, naïve? She was downright stupid, yeah! Superficial, nothing in her brain, no knowledge. She couldn't even string three words together properly in French, so in English! Can you imagine? And Kevin chose her?! He married this dummy in less than two months and then took her to live on one of the most beautiful continents in the world. I taught Kevin everything! I gave him seven years of my life! I lost my job for him! We travelled, we went to museums, we went out. I supported him in his studies to become an engineer. We were happy! And then, from one day to the next, he dumps me for this brat. No! Unacceptable! I knew about Kevin's expatriation plans, since he was going to Australia with me. I asked about his plans and I put ads for home language courses in the neighbourhood mailboxes. Naturally, Chloe contacted me. Kevin didn't make the connection. I studied Chloe for a while. I wanted to know why he had fallen in love with her. I listened to her whining about her ex. **(To Quentin):** "If you hadn't been such a jerk, she would have stayed with you! You idiot!" This morning we decided that I would come early for class. 7.30, because she had to leave at 8.30 for an appointment at the town hall in connection with her passport. I had not slept well, I was tired. She once again barked out the TH in English. It's not difficult to put your tongue between your teeth to pronounce it properly! I pulled the pin! I took one of the kitchen knives from the service that she had got as a wedding present, and...I cut up the turkey (she laughed).

JEANINE P.: «Well, can I go now?»

INVESTIGATION 8 : CHLOE

Note-taking

Don't hesitate to tell us what you liked the most in this investigation or what you would have liked to find in it, by leaving a review about your order (we may take it into account in the next edition)!

In the same collection:

- Riddles for Smart Teens, published in April 2022

- Quiz for Smart Teens, published in April 2023

Made in the USA
Columbia, SC
09 January 2025